maybe

Published by Bushel & Peck Books, a family-run publishing house in Fresno, California, that believes
in uplifting children with the highest standards of art, music, literature, and ideas. Find beautiful
books for gifted young minds at www.bushelandpeckbooks.com.

Type set in IM Fell English Pro and Braisetto.
Vintage artwork sourced from Rawpixel.com and Wikimedia Commons;
border licensed from Shutterstock.com.

Bushel & Peck Books is dedicated to fighting illiteracy all over the world. For every book we sell,
we donate one to a child in need—book for book. To nominate a school or organization to
receive free books, please visit www.bushelandpeckbooks.com.

LCCN: 2022930349
ISBN: 9781638191018

First Edition

Printed in the United States

10 9 8 7 6 5 4 3 2 1

maybe

A MINDFULNESS TALE

ADAPTED FROM A
TRADITIONAL FOLKTALE

BUSHEL
& PECK
BOOKS

INTRODUCTION

As you read this story, think about what the farmer says whenever something happens. Could good things be bad? Could bad things be good? Is it possible to not judge an event as *either* good or bad? A key to peaceful mindfulness is learning to accept rather than to judge. After you read the story, think about things that have happened in your life. Can you open your mind and fully accept them without judgment? Read on—the farmer shows the way!

Once upon a time,
deep in the shadow
of the mountain, there
lived a wise old farmer.

*A*ll day long, the farmer labored with his son planting rice in the deep, rich mud made by the rains from heaven.

But one day, the rains didn't stop. Water poured from the sky, the river overflowed, and the farmer and his son had to work all night long to save the crop.

"How terrible!" mewed the cat.

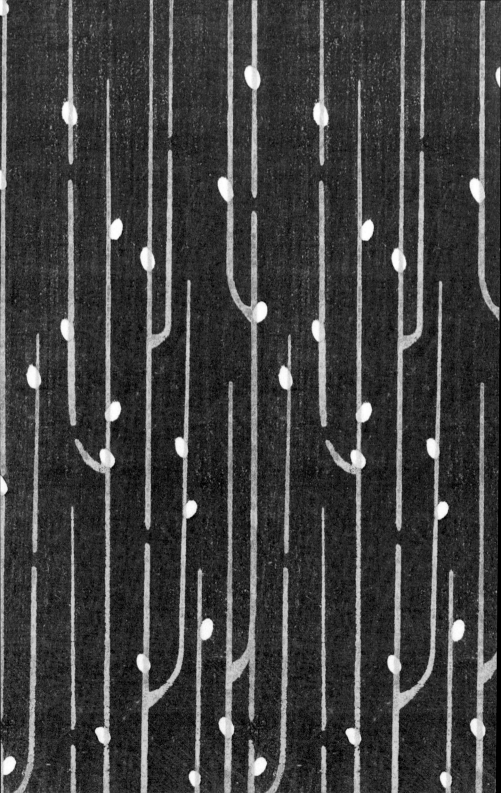

"Maybe," said the farmer.

When the waters receded, it was discovered that the farmer's fields were filled with thousands of fish—enough to feed his family for a whole year.

"How fortunate!" chattered the monkey.

"Maybe," said the farmer.

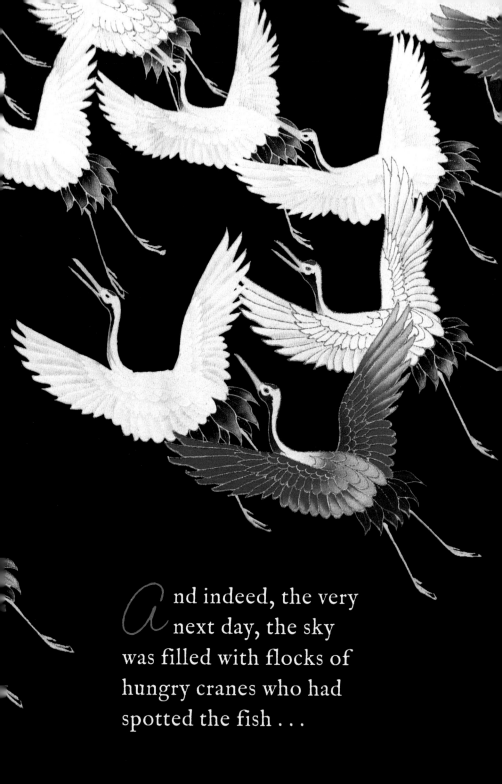

*a*nd indeed, the very next day, the sky was filled with flocks of hungry cranes who had spotted the fish . . .

. . . and the farmer's rice
was completely trampled
by their excited feet.

"How awful!"
cried the eagle.

"Maybe," said the farmer.

The next morning, a royal scribe came through town. When he spotted the empty field, he offered the farmer fifteen gold ingots for the land to build a royal barracks.

"How wonderful!" hooted the owl.

"Maybe," said the farmer.

He traveled to the city and bought a new horse for his son with the gold from the royal scribe. But the very next day, the horse ran away.

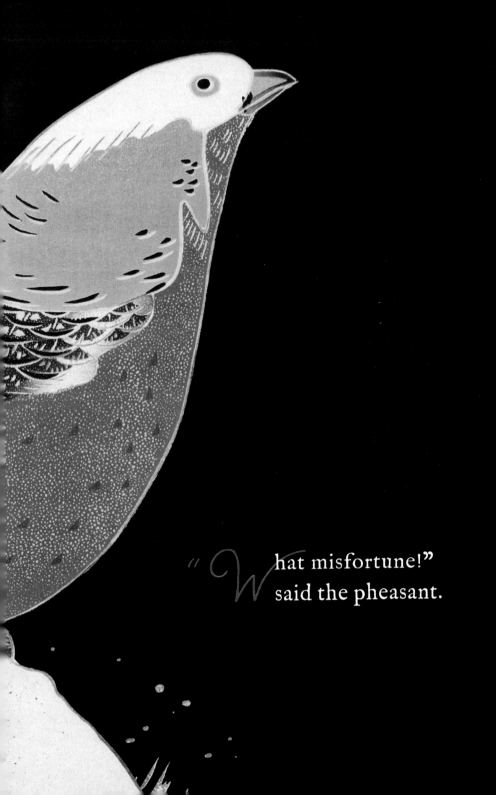

"What misfortune!" said the pheasant.

"Maybe," said the farmer.

*L*ate that evening
the horse returned,
bringing twenty more
wild horses with it.

"What great
luck!"
crowed the rooster.

"Maybe," said the farmer.

As the farmer's son was training one of the wild horses that night, the horse kicked the son hard and broke his leg.

"What a shame!" growled the tiger.

"Maybe," said the farmer.

And indeed, when the army came to the village to use the new barracks, the Emperor commanded all the young men to enlist . . .

. . . but the farmer's son was excused on account of his lame leg.

" What a blessing!"
said all the village.

"Maybe," said
the farmer . . .

BUSHEL
& PECK
BOOKS

ABOUT BUSHEL & PECK BOOKS

*B*ushel & Peck Books is a children's publishing house with a special mission. Through our Book-for-Book Promise™, we donate one book to kids in need for every book we sell. Our beautiful books are given to kids through schools, libraries, local neighborhoods, shelters, nonprofits, and also to many selfless organizations that are working hard to make a difference. So thank you for purchasing this book! Because of you, another book will make its way into the hands of a child who needs it most.

NOMINATE A SCHOOL OR ORGANIZATION TO RECEIVE FREE BOOKS

*D*o you know a school, library, or organization that could use some free books for their kids? We'd love to help! Please fill out the nomination form on our website, and we'll do everything we can to make something happen.

www.bushelandpeckbooks.com/pages/
nominate-a-school-or-organization

If you liked this book, please leave a review online at your favorite retailer. Honest reviews spread the word about Bushel & Peck—and help us make better books, too!

Printed in the United States
by Baker & Taylor Publisher Services